Super Explorers

WEIRD OCEAN CREATURES

Tamara Hartson

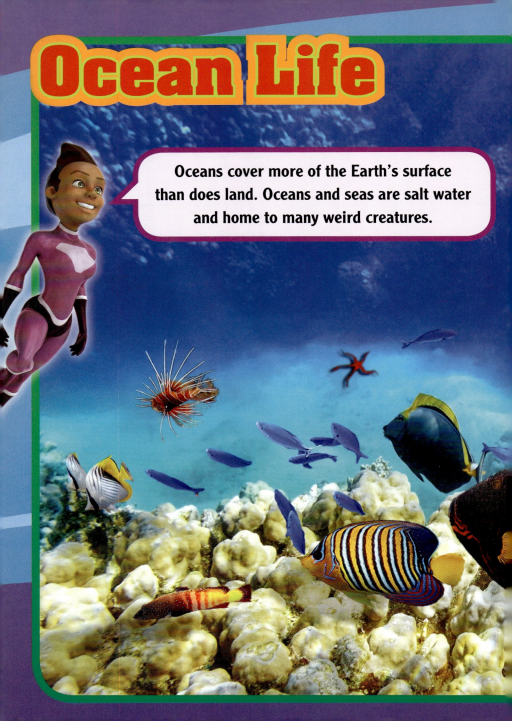

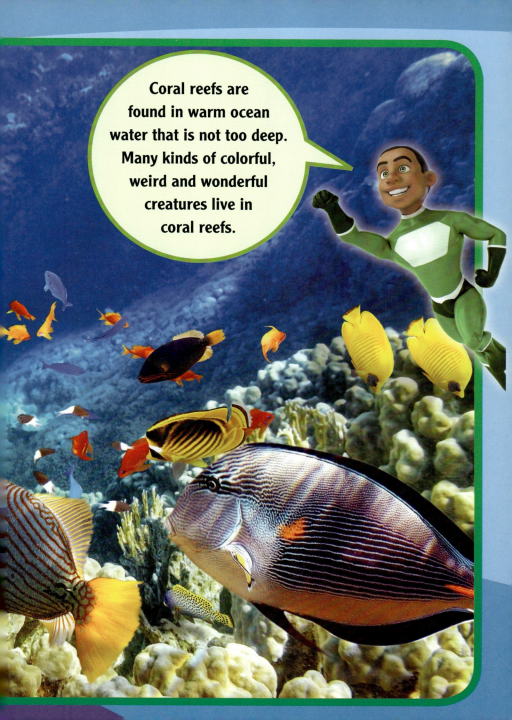

Sea Pen

Sea pens look like plants growing on the ocean floor, but they are actually animals! One pen is really a colony of many polyps, which are like tiny jellyfish with tentacles.

Purple Sea Pen

Sea pens get their name because they look like old-fashioned feather pens in an ink pot.

Jellyfish

Moon Jelly

Jellyfish are **umbrella-shaped** animals that live in the ocean. They have **tentacles** with thousands of tiny stingers that stun their prey, such as fish or shrimp.

Deep-red Jellyfish

The most **deadly venom** in the world is from a **box jellyfish!** Stings from box jellies are dangerous to humans.

Box Jellyfish

Cauliflower Jellyfish

Jellyfish have been alive for about 700 million years. They were living even before dinosaurs!

Pink Meanie

The pink meanie is a species of giant jellyfish that feeds on other jellyfish! Little fish that are immune to the jellyfish's sting often swim under it for safety from predators. The little fish attract predators that the pink meanie then catches and eats. The little fish get to eat bits of the catch as well.

Leafy Sea Dragon

Leafy sea dragons are related to seahorses and pipefish. These fish live only on the southern coast of Australia. Leafy sea dragons have long, leafy branches on their bodies that help them **hide in seaweed.**

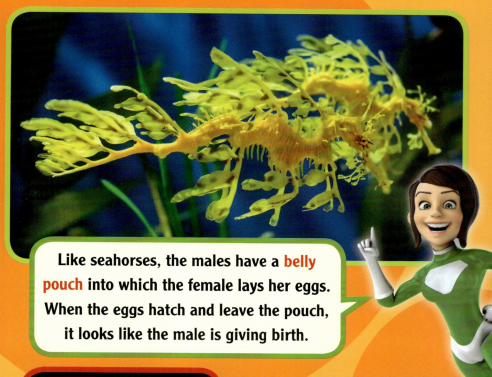

Like seahorses, the males have a **belly pouch** into which the female lays her eggs. When the eggs hatch and leave the pouch, it looks like the male is giving birth.

Even though they are called **dragons,** the largest leafy sea dragon is no bigger than a piece of writing paper.

Sea Slugs

Sea slugs are also known as nudibranchs. They are like snails that no longer have shells. Sea slugs are mollusks, a group that includes snails, clams, octopuses and squid. There are thousands of different sea slugs!

Spanish Shawl

Hypselodoris kanga

Sea slugs are carnivores. They eat other animals like sea anemones, jellyfish and even other sea slugs!

Glossodoris atromarginata

Variable Neon Slug

Chromodoris annae

Sea slugs have feathery **external gills** for breathing that look a bit like tentacles.

Blue Dragon

The blue dragon feeds on jellyfish, even those with deadly stingers. The sea slugs store the stingers in their own bodies, making these creatures painful and dangerous to touch.

Narwhal

The **narwhal** is sometimes called the **unicorn of the sea** because it has what looks like a unicorn horn on its head. The horn is actually a **tusk,** which means it is a tooth that sticks out from the jaw.

Narwhals in a Pod

Narwhals in a Pod

Narwhals are whales that live in the Arctic. They travel in groups called pods.

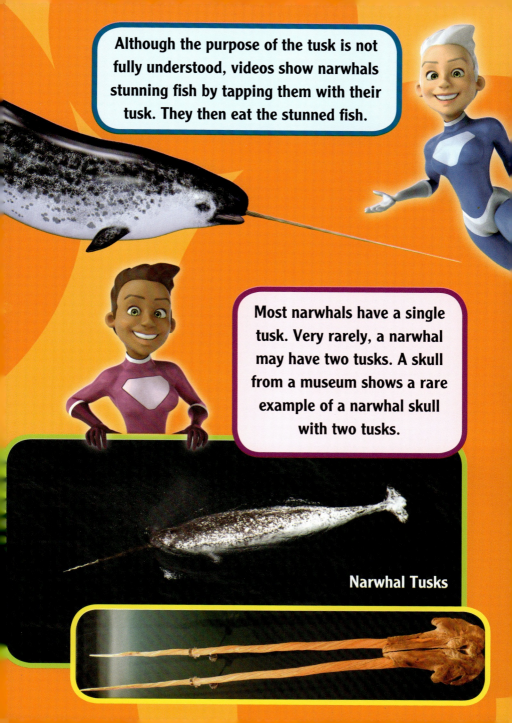

Salp

Chain of Salps

Salps are unusual looking creatures that can live alone or in long chains. A single salp is shaped like a barrel. Salps feed on tiny ocean creatures called **plankton.**

Ring of Salps

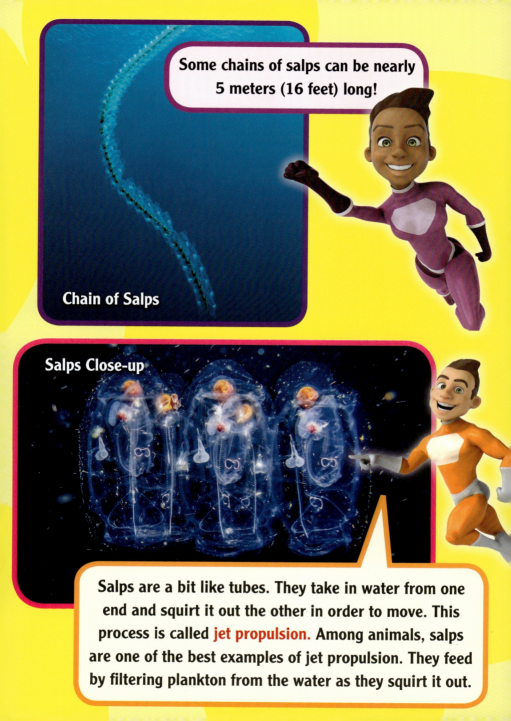

Porcupinefish

Spotted Porcupinefish

Porcupinefish are found in warm oceans around the world. They live in **coral reefs.** Sometimes hundreds or even thousands can be found together in a **school.**

Black-blotched Porcupinefish

Porcupinefish can rapidly swallow water or air to **inflate themselves.** This protects them from predators such as sharks and dolphins because their spines stick straight out. Most predators will avoid trying to eat a puffed up porcupinefish!

Spotted Porcupinefish

With long legs and small bodies, **sea spiders** look like real spiders. They are not true spiders, but they are more closely related to spiders than to either insects or crustaceans (crabs and shrimp).

Sea spiders move by either walking or swimming. When they swim, they wave their legs up and down as if they are crawling through the water.

Swimming Sea Spider

Sea spiders have tiny bodies in relation to their legs. Their legs absorb oxygen from the water, so that means they breathe with their legs!

Sea Spiders

The **blue whale** is the largest animal ever known. It is even heavier than the largest dinosaurs! Blue whales are mammals, which means they are warm-blooded, give birth to live young and nurse their young with milk. A newborn calf is as big as an adult hippopotamus!

A blue whale's heart weighs 180 kilograms (400 pounds). That's about as heavy as a piano!

Blue Whale

Like all other whales and dolphins, blue whales breathe air. They come to the surface to exhale and inhale air through the blowholes on the top of their heads.

Blowhole

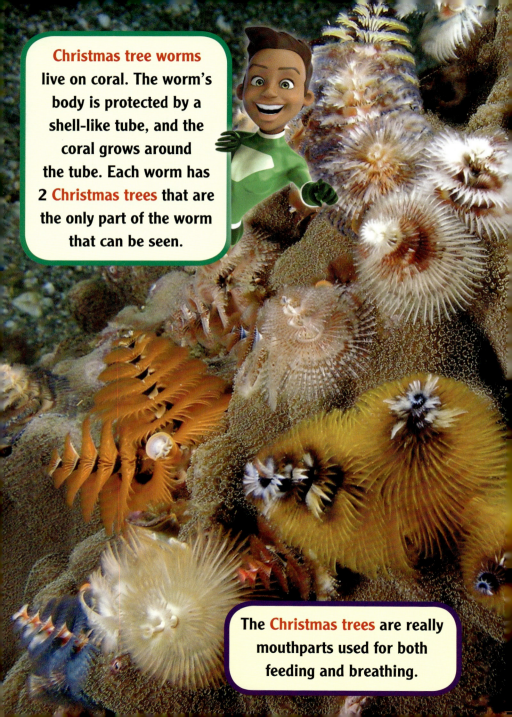

Christmas tree worms live on coral. The worm's body is protected by a shell-like tube, and the coral grows around the tube. Each worm has 2 **Christmas trees** that are the only part of the worm that can be seen.

The **Christmas trees** are really mouthparts used for both feeding and breathing.

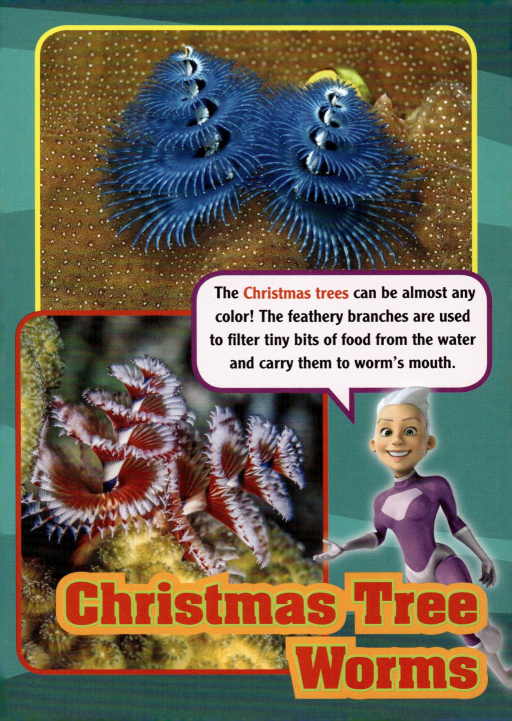

Sea Angels

Sea angels are small, transparent sea slugs that live in all oceans. They can be as small as a blueberry or as big as an apricot.

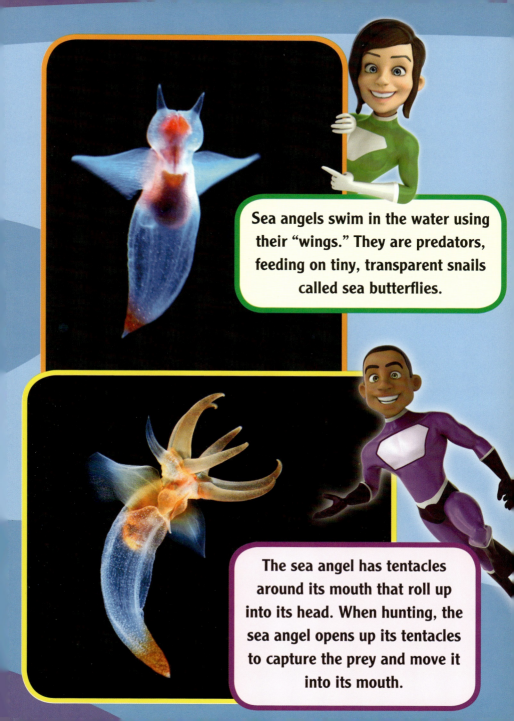

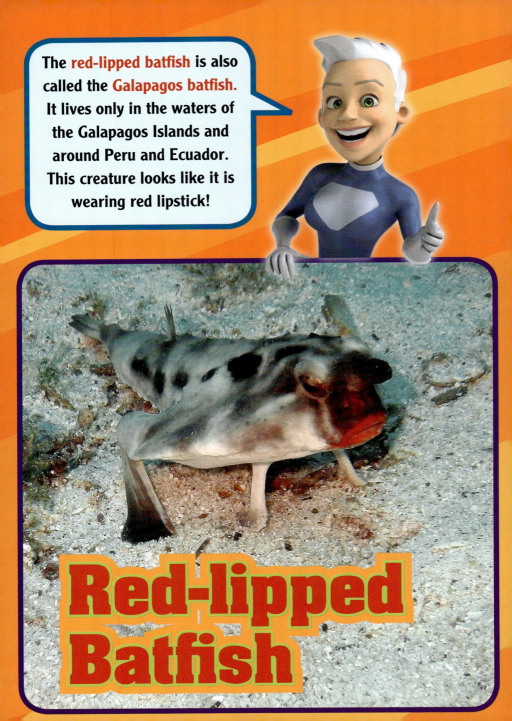

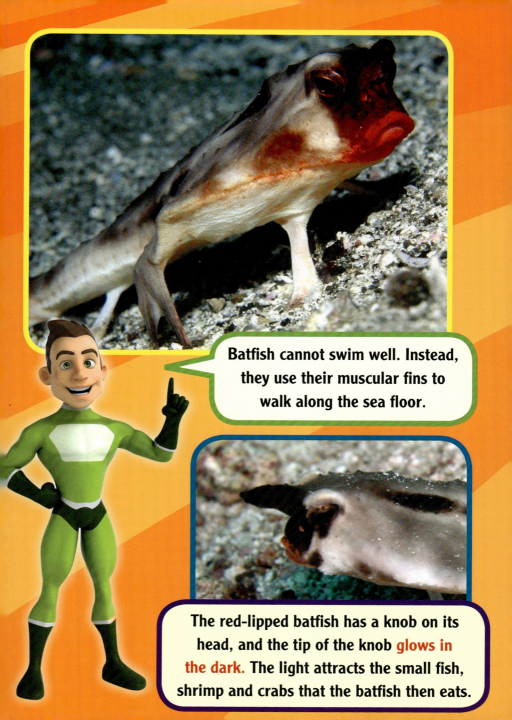

Batfish cannot swim well. Instead, they use their muscular fins to walk along the sea floor.

The red-lipped batfish has a knob on its head, and the tip of the knob **glows in the dark**. The light attracts the small fish, shrimp and crabs that the batfish then eats.

Fangtooth Moray

Moray eels are often found in coral reefs. They have 2 sets of jaws to help them catch their prey and pull it into their throats. Some morays wait in crevices for prey to approach, while others actively hunt.

Zebra Moray

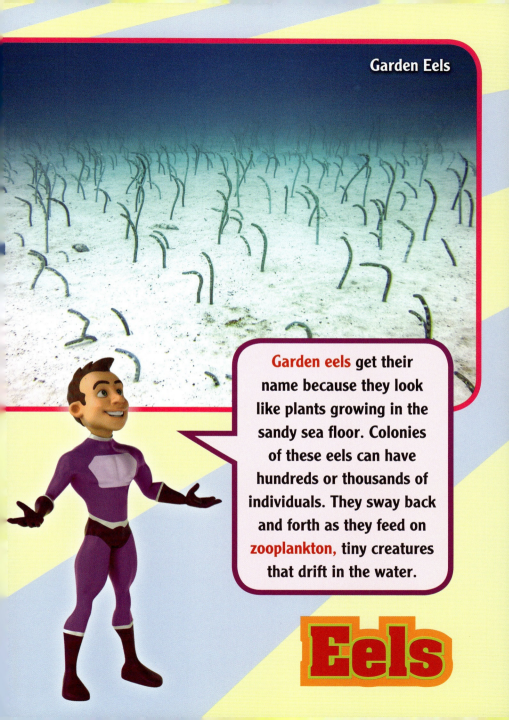

Garden Eels

Garden eels get their name because they look like plants growing in the sandy sea floor. Colonies of these eels can have hundreds or thousands of individuals. They sway back and forth as they feed on **zooplankton,** tiny creatures that drift in the water.

Eels

Sea Urchins

Although it looks like an underwater cactus, the **sea urchin** is really an animal! These creatures feed mainly on algae, a tiny, plant-like organism.

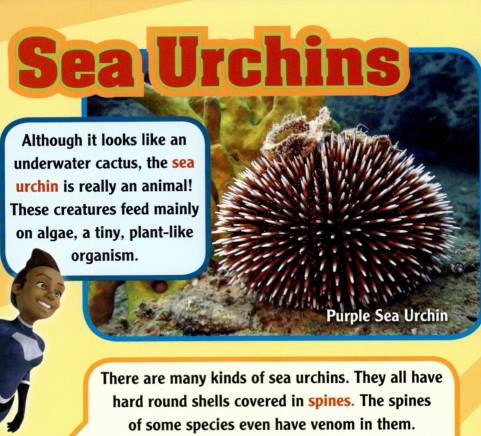

Purple Sea Urchin

There are many kinds of sea urchins. They all have hard round shells covered in **spines.** The spines of some species even have venom in them. Sometimes small fish hide in the spines for safety.

Long-spined Sea Urchin

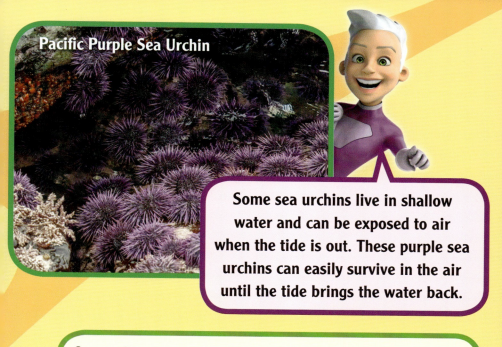

Pacific Purple Sea Urchin

Some sea urchins live in shallow water and can be exposed to air when the tide is out. These purple sea urchins can easily survive in the air until the tide brings the water back.

Sea urchins are also covered in **tentacles** with tiny suction cups at the tip. The tentacles on the bottom of the urchin are called **tube feet** and are used for walking slowly. Both the spines and tentacles are sensitive to light, which is good because the urchin lacks eyes!

Red Sea Urchin

Carrier Crab

Protection from predators is a full-time job for many ocean creatures. The **carrier crab** has developed a creative way to defend itself. Since most predators avoid spiky sea urchins, this crab carries one around on its back!

This crab uses its back two pairs of legs to hold onto the sea urchin. It usually keeps any one sea urchin on its back only for a little while. The sea urchin also benefits by being carried a long distance to new feeding areas.

Bobbit Worms

Bobbit worms live in burrows on the ocean floor. They look and act more like aliens in a scary movie than worms!

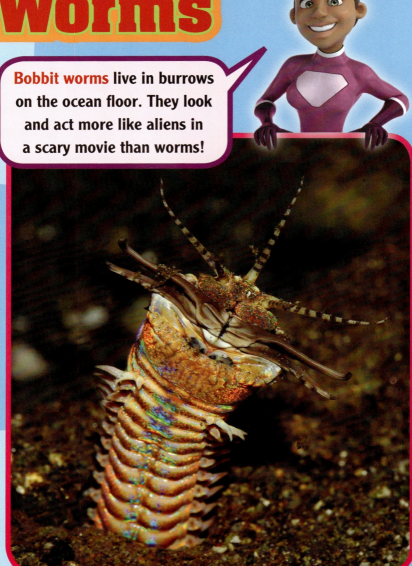

Bobbit worms remain mostly hidden in their burrows until prey such as small fish or shrimp pass near their sensitive antennae. When they sense their prey, they lunge out of their burrows and crush the animal in their strong jaws.

Bobbit worms can be very long and thin. The longest ever recorded was nearly 300 centimeters (118 inches) long!

Mandarin Fish

Mandarin fish are small fish that live in tropical reefs. They feed on small invertebrates and fish eggs.

Instead of scales, these fish have a layer of smelly, bitter slime over their bodies. Their intense colors warn predators that they taste bad!

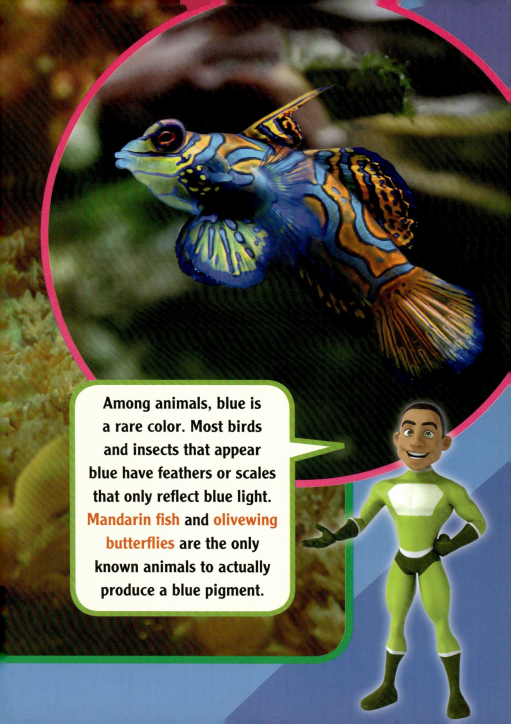

Among animals, blue is a rare color. Most birds and insects that appear blue have feathers or scales that only reflect blue light. **Mandarin fish** and **olivewing butterflies** are the only known animals to actually produce a blue pigment.

Basking Shark

The second largest shark in the world, the **basking shark**, is about as long as a school bus! This shark has a huge mouth, but it poses no danger to humans.

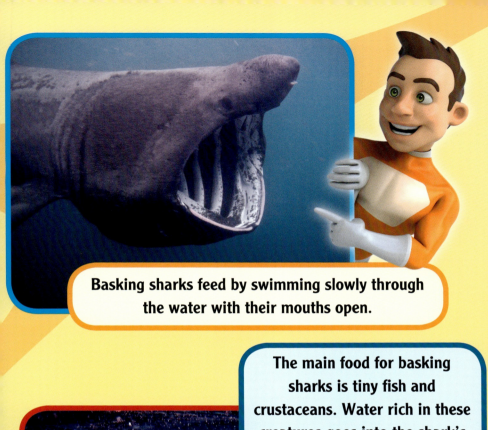

Basking sharks feed by swimming slowly through the water with their mouths open.

The main food for basking sharks is tiny fish and crustaceans. Water rich in these creatures goes into the shark's mouth. The water exits through the gills at the back of the mouth, but the tiny creatures are trapped and swallowed.

Miniature Melo Bubble Snail

Bubble snails are a group of snails that have large bodies and small shells. Like bubbles, their shells are round and very thin.

Miniature Melo Bubble Snail

Rose Petal Bubble Snail

Snails are **mollusks** and are related to sea slugs, squid and octopuses. These mollusks have a large, muscular "foot" used for creeping along the ocean floor. The foot of the bubble snail is colorful and so large that the snail cannot retract into its shell like other snails.

Rose Petal Bubble Snail

Bubble Snails

Decorator Crab

Crab covered in bits of algae

Decorator crabs are a group of crustaceans that cover themselves with bits of seaweed, shells, sponges or anemones. When the crab is completely covered, it is hard to see. This is called **camouflage**.

Crab covered in sponges

Crab covered in tiny anemones

Some decorator crabs cover themselves with stinging anemones. The anemones both camouflage the crab and protect it with their stinging tentacles. The anemones get to feed on bits food left over by the crab.

This crab has attached a leafy plant to its head and green bits to its body. When it stays still, it looks just like seaweed!

Crab covered in seaweed

The **peacock flounder** has blue dots and circles that resemble the feathers of a peacock.

Flounders begin life as ordinary fish that swim upright in the water with eyes on either side of their head. As they grow, one eye slowly moves to the other side, so both eyes end up on the same side and the fish can lay flat on the ocean floor. Their mouth doesn't move, so the flounder has a quirky, lopsided face.

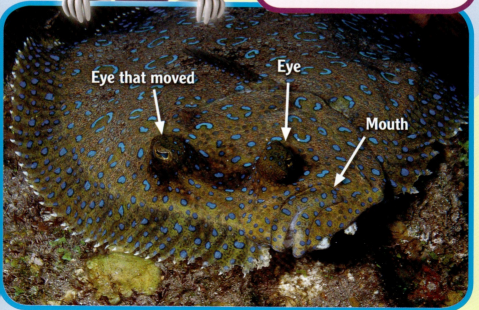

Eye that moved

Eye

Mouth

Japanese Spider Crab

The **Japanese Spider Crab** is the largest **crustacean** in the world. Its legs can stretch out so the creature is as long as a car!

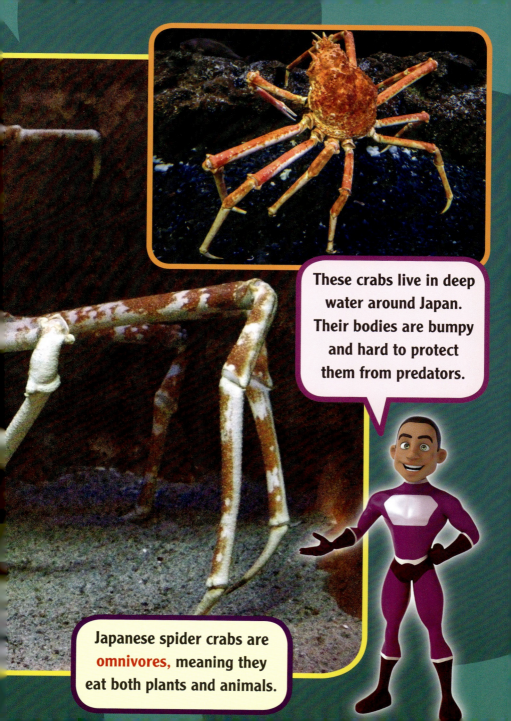

Hammerhead Shark

Hammerhead sharks are found throughout the world in coastal waters. During the day they swim together in schools, and at night they hunt alone. Hammerheads range in size from as small as a dog to as large as pickup truck.

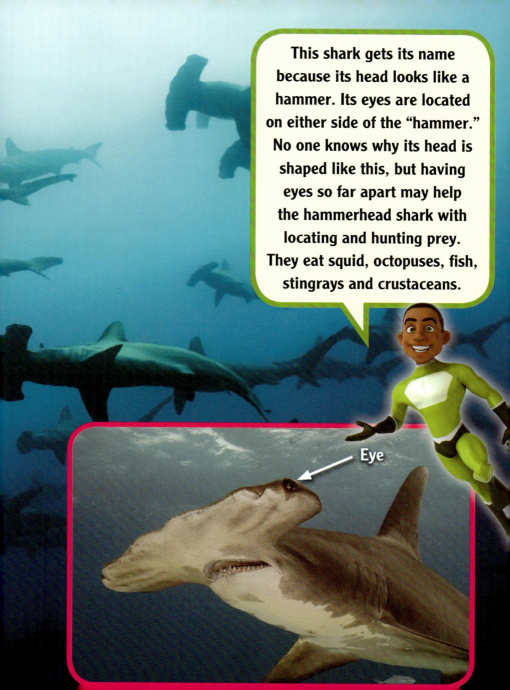

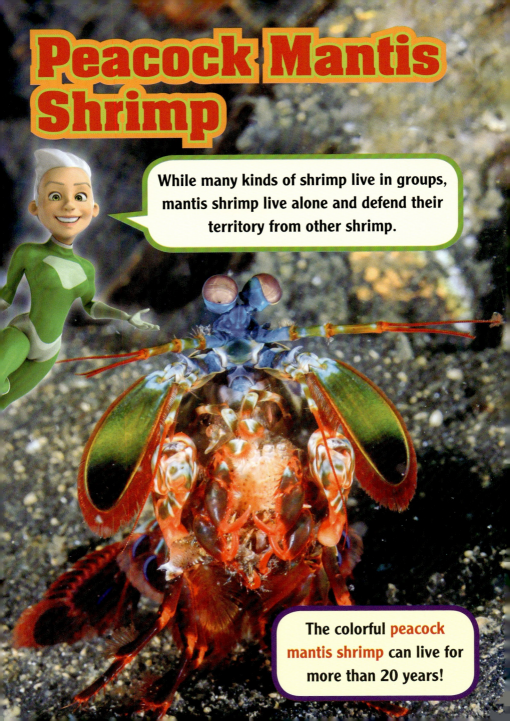

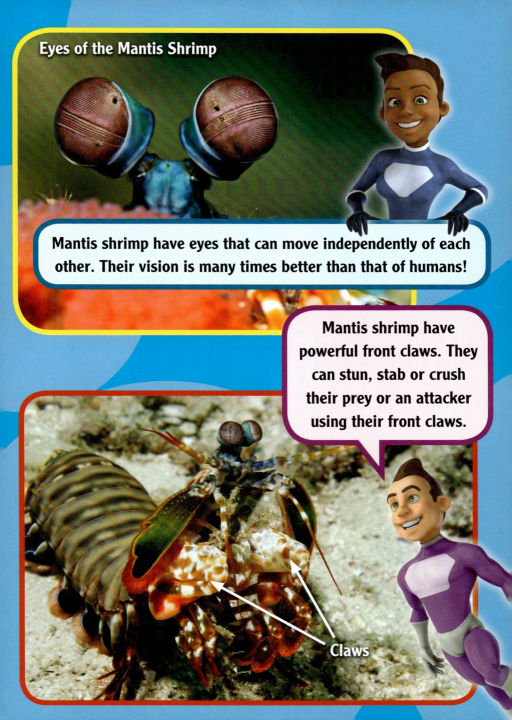

Lionfish

Lionfish are a group of fishes that look like they have long feathers. The "feathers" are the individual spines of their fins, and each is tipped with poison!

Red Lionfish

Sea Anemone

Sea anemones are animals that are related to coral and jellyfish. Although they look like they are stationary, anemones can slowly creep over the surface to which they are attached. Their tentacles have stingers to stun their prey, such as small crabs and fish. A sea anemone's mouth is in the center of its tentacles.

Orange Anemone

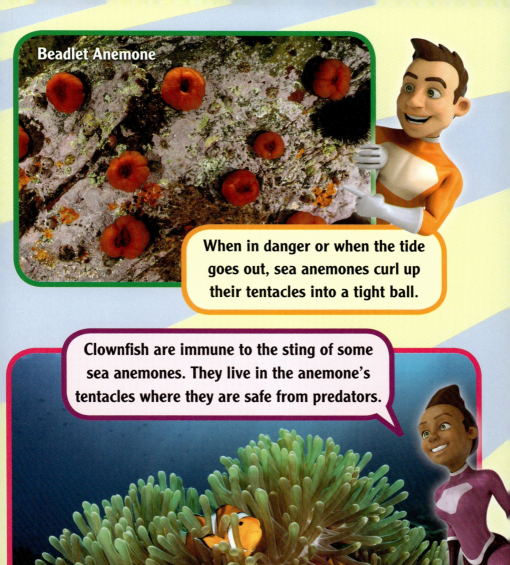

Dumbo Octopus

The Dumbo octopus gets its name from its large "ears" that resemble those of Disney's Dumbo the Elephant. Located above their eyes, these "ears" are actually fins that they use for swimming.

Crinoids

Swimming crinoid

Crinoids are **echinoderms** that are related to sea urchins and sand dollars. They have legs called **cirri** that help them walk or attach to a hard surface. They look a bit like walking ferns! Crinoids can also swim by waving their feather-like arms up and down.

Elegant Feather Star

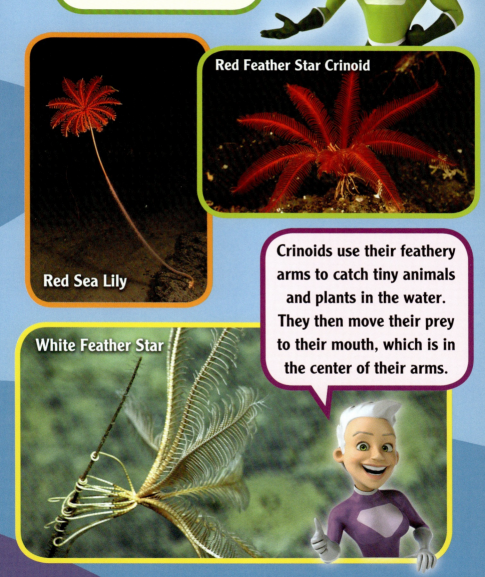

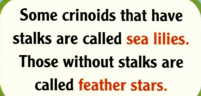

Some crinoids that have stalks are called **sea lilies.** Those without stalks are called **feather stars.**

Red Feather Star Crinoid

Red Sea Lily

White Feather Star

Crinoids use their feathery arms to catch tiny animals and plants in the water. They then move their prey to their mouth, which is in the center of their arms.

Ocean Sunfish

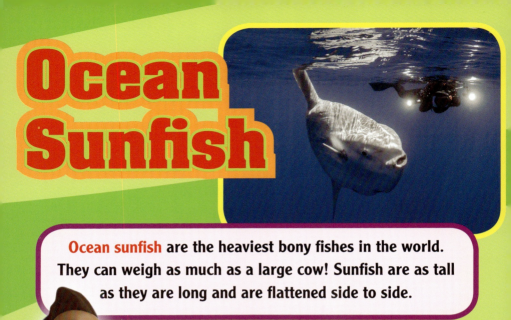

Ocean sunfish are the heaviest bony fishes in the world. They can weigh as much as a large cow! Sunfish are as tall as they are long and are flattened side to side.

Basking sunfish

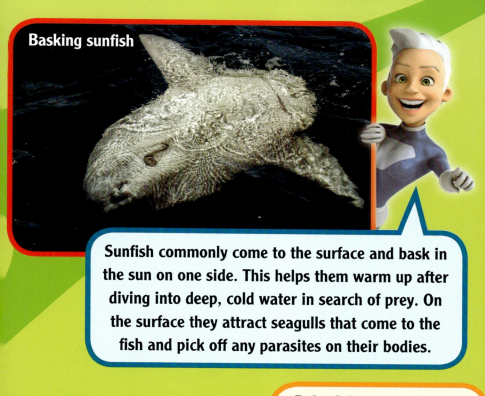

Sunfish commonly come to the surface and bask in the sun on one side. This helps them warm up after diving into deep, cold water in search of prey. On the surface they attract seagulls that come to the fish and pick off any parasites on their bodies.

Sunfish fry

Baby fish are call **fish fry.** Sunfish fry are about the size of a pencil eraser and are shaped like stars!

Pink See-through Fantasia

Discovered in the year 2007, the **pink see-through fantasia** is a kind of deep sea cucumber related to sea urchins and starfish. Its other names are **Spanish dancer** and **headless chicken monster!**

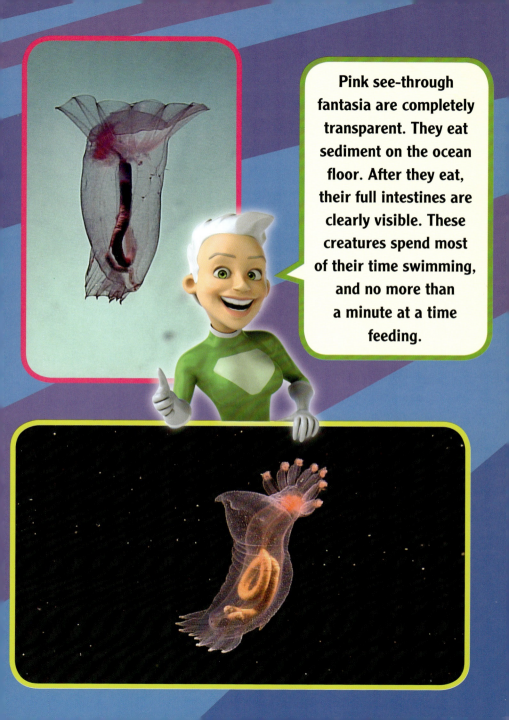

© 2019 Super Explorers

Printed in China

All rights reserved. No part of this work covered by the copyrights hereon may be reproduced or used in any form or by any means—graphic, electronic or mechanical—without the prior written permission of the publisher, except for reviewers, who may quote brief passages. Any request for photocopying, recording, taping or storage on information retrieval systems of any part of this work shall be directed in writing to the publisher.

The Publisher: Super Explorers is an imprint of Blue Bike Books

Library and Archives Canada Cataloguing in Publication

Title: Weird ocean creatures / Tamara Hartson.
Names: Hartson, Tamara, 1974– author.
Identifiers: Canadiana 20190218762 | ISBN 9781926700144 (softcover)
Subjects: LCSH: Deep-sea animals—Juvenile literature.
Classification: LCC QL125.5 .H37 2020 | DDC j591.77/9—dc23

Front cover credit: crisod/Getty Images.

Back cover credits: johnandersonphoto/Getty Images, NOAA, jenny/Wikimedia Commons.

Photo Credits: From Thinkstock: atese 4a; barbaraaaa 9b; cbpix 10a; Cindy Chow 9a; FtLaudGirl 17; goir 4b; joebelanger 10b; N-sky 16b; naturediver 5a; Oleksii Spesyvtsev 16a; olga_steckel 7b; tingfen 8b; williamhc 9c. From Getty Images: _jure 30a; Arrlxx 46-47; atese 28b, 53a; bearacreative 52; ct johnson 44b; Damocean 55a; David Haintz 18b; demarfa 28a; fusaromike 31a; Howard Chen 49a; IAM-photography 29; izanbar 61a; Janos 15a, 48-49; johnandersonphoto 23b, 42b; Jupiterimages 27a; kata716 25a; kateafter 47a; LeventKonuk 23a; Magnus Larsson 55b; marrio31 36-37; Matt_Potenski 45; Maurizio Lanini 11b; Michael Zeigler 60a; naturediver 31b, 54; oksanavg 51b; prill 30b; Rebecca-Belleni-Photography 39a, 39b; RiberiodosSantos 19b; RLSPHOTO 24b; S.Rohrlach 41b; scubaluna 51a; serajace 15b; TuTheLens 24a; Vac1 13a; VitalyEdush 3-4; WhitcombeRD 50; Zeamonkey 33b. From Wikimedia Commons: Alexander Vasenin 58a; Bernard Picton 19a; Chika Watanabe 10c; Chris Gotschalk 38; Derek Keats 7a; G. David Johnson 61b; Guido Gautsch 6c; Hans Hillewaert 6a; Jenny 34; Luc Viatour 37a; Nathalie Rodrigues 40b; Nhobgood 11a; Nick Hobgood 5b, 22, 43a; NOAA 6b, 21b; Peter Southwood 14b; Rein Ketelaars 26; Samuel Chow 41a; Seascapeza 58b; soebe.jpg 13c; Steve Childs 40a; Sylke Rohrlach 8a, 11c, 32; The High Fin Sperm Whale 53b; пресс-служба ПАО "Газпром нефть" 12b, 13b. From Flickr: Bernard DUPONT 33a; Daniel Dietrich 42a; Ken Traub 35b; Lars Plougmann 14a; Lucy Rickards 27b; NOAA 12a, 18a, 20-21, 56, 57a, 57b, 59a, 59b, 59c, 62a, 62b, 63a, 63b; Rickard Zerpe 35a; Silke Baron 43b. Alexander Semenov 25b.

Superhero Illustrations: julos/Thinkstock.

Produced with the assistance of the Government of Alberta.

We acknowledge the financial support of the Government of Canada.

Nous reconnaissons l'appui financier du gouvernement du Canada.

PC: 38-1